Growing Up on a Farm
Responsibilities and Issues

Title List

Getting Ready for the Fair: Crafts, Projects, and Prize-Winning Animals

Growing Up on a Farm: Responsibilities and Issues

Migrant Youth: Falling Between the Cracks

Rural Crime and Poverty: Violence, Drugs, and Other Issues

Rural Teens and Animal Raising: Large and Small Pets

Rural Teens and Nature: Conservation and Wildlife Rehabilitation

Rural Teens on the Move:
Cars, Motorcycles, and Off-Road Vehicles

Teen Life Among the Amish and Other Alternative Communities:
Choosing a Lifestyle

Teen Life on Reservations and in First Nation Communities:
Growing Up Native

Teen Minorities in Rural North America: Growing Up Different

Teens and Rural Education: Opportunities and Challenges

Teens and Rural Sports: Rodeos, Horses, Hunting, and Fishing

Teens Who Make a Difference in Rural Communities:
Youth Outreach Organizations and Community Action

Growing Up on a Farm
Responsibilities and Issues

by Peter Sieling

Mason Crest Publishers

Philadelphia

Mason Crest Publishers Inc.
370 Reed Road
Broomall, Pennsylvania 19008
(866) MCP-BOOK (toll free)
www.masoncrest.com

First printing
1 2 3 4 5 6 7 8 9 10
ISBN 978-1-4222-0011-7 (series)

Library of Congress Cataloging-in-Publication Data

Sieling, Peter.
  Growing up on a farm : responsibilities and issues / by Peter Sieling.
      p. cm. — (Youth in rural North America)
  Includes bibliographical references and index.
  ISBN 978-1-4222-0012-4
  1. Farm life—United States—Juvenile literature. 2. Rural youth—United States—Juvenile literature. 3. Agriculture—United States—Juvenile literature. I. Title. II. Series.
  HT421.S369 2007
  307.720973—dc22
                                    2005033177

Cover and interior design by MK Bassett-Harvey.
Produced by Harding House Publishing Service, Inc.
www.hardinghousepages.com

Cover image design by Peter Culotta.
Cover photography by iStock Photography (James Pauls).
Printed in Malaysia by Phoenix Press.

Contents

Introduction

by Celeste Carmichael

Results of a survey published by the Kellogg Foundation reveal that most people consider growing up in the country to be idyllic. And it's true that growing up in a rural environment does have real benefits. Research indicates that families in rural areas consistently have more traditional values, and communities are more closely knit. Rural youth spend more time than their urban counterparts in contact with agriculture and nature. Often youth are responsible for gardens and farm animals, and they benefit from both their sense of responsibility and their understanding of the natural world. Studies also indicate that rural youth are more engaged in their communities, working to improve society and local issues. And let us not forget the psychological and aesthetic benefits of living in a serene rural environment!

The advantages of rural living cannot be overlooked—but neither can the challenges. Statistics from around the country show that children in a rural environment face many of the same difficulties that are typically associated with children living in cities, and they fare worse than urban kids on several key indicators of positive youth development. For example, rural youth are more likely than their urban counterparts to use drugs and alcohol. Many of the problems facing rural youth are exacerbated by isolation, lack of jobs (for both parents and teens), and lack of support services for families in rural communities.

When most people hear the word "rural," they instantly think "farms." Actually, however, less than 12 percent of the population in rural areas make their livings through agriculture. Instead, service jobs are the top industry in rural North America. The lack of opportunities for higher paying jobs can trigger many problems: persistent poverty, lower educational standards, limited access to health care, inadequate housing, underemployment of teens, and lack of extracurricular possibilities. Additionally, the lack of—or in some cases surge of—diverse populations in rural communities presents its own set of challenges for youth and communities. All these concerns lead to the greatest threat to rural communities: the mass exodus of the post–high school population. Teens relocate for educational, recreational, and job opportunities, leaving their hometown indefinitely deficient in youth capital.

This series of books offers an in-depth examination of both the pleasures and challenges for rural youth. Understanding the realities is the first step to expanding the options for rural youth and increasing the likelihood of positive youth development.

CHAPTER 1

Young Farmer: How One Teenager Established His Own Farm

Andy had wanted to farm since kindergarten. He lived with his family in a small town until age fourteen, when his father died, and then Andy moved back to the old family farm with his mother, brother, and sister. He found the old Farmall tractor still ran. Rusty farm implements sat in the hedgerows. The fields lay *fallow*. As Andy explained, "After Dad died, we had the farm. Why not farm it?"

Fallow fields are not planted for a year or two to allow the soil to rest and become fertile again.

Daisy, the Miracle Cow

Andy describes how he acquired his first cow: "We were just about to move back to the farm when one of Dad's old friends offered me a calf. Bull calves were going cheap then, around five dollars apiece. The farmer said one of his cows was expecting. If I wanted a calf, he'd rather give it to me than sell it.

"Later he called. 'You got twins!' I was excited to think I was going to have two calves, but as things turned out, the bull calf got caught on his rope and died. The surviving heifer was a twin to a bull. That means it doesn't breed, or at least the chances are almost zero, so I planned to raise her for meat. We put her in the back of the station wagon and took her up to the farm. I found another bull calf, though, so I had two to raise after all: Daisy and Ferdinand. I fixed the old barn and put up an electric fence."

Raising beef calves is much easier than dairy cows. You don't need expensive milking equipment. Daisy decided to surprise Andy, though.

"When Daisy was fourteen or fifteen months old, we noticed her bellowing a lot, which seemed odd. That's the age when a heifer 'goes into heat' or is ready to breed. I was making money working on a neighboring farm, so I knew the breeder. He came over and checked Daisy. When he found she had all the right parts, he bred her. Two or three months later, he came back because I thought she was in heat again. He felt around and told me to call the vet. The vet came and looked. Sure enough, there was a calf in her.

"I was home the day she delivered. By that time I'd worked for several farmers and had helped deliver lots of calves, so I knew what to expect. I looked across the road, and she looked like she was getting ready. Later, I saw her licking her new heifer calf. I named the calf Darla."

Once a cow calves, it's time to milk. Andy soon learned to appreciate the automatic milking equipment he used at work on a dairy farm.

"I hand milked her for a long time, twice a day. You only needed a thumb and your first finger, but my arms started hurting like crazy. At first she kicked, but she got used to it. Darla started drinking a lot of milk. I was glad because I didn't have to milk quite as much.

"Milking gave me strong arms and hands. I remember my older cousin Dan asking me to squeeze his hand. 'I'll tell you when to stop,' he said. I squeezed his hand and he squeaked, 'Okay, stop!'

"'You weren't even half there, were you?' he asked, rubbing his sore hand.

"'Probably not,' I answered.

"I never actually weaned Darla, although I tried separating them. We had an old gate that I thought was in pretty good shape. I put them in separate pastures with the gate between. Darla just dropped her head, ran straight into the gate, and boom! It blew into a million pieces. I tried putting a spiked muzzle on her. When she tried to nurse, the spikes were supposed to poke Daisy in the udder. It didn't work. Darla managed to twist the muzzle around so it wouldn't poke her mother."

Learning the Hard Way

Working for other farmers provided valuable experience and knowledge. Andy still had to learn many things himself, though.

"I cut my own fence posts and put up an electric fence. I really needed three or four strands of wire, not one, which was what I had. The cows weren't bad, but they escaped whenever they felt like it and wandered over to neighboring farms. The farmer who rented our fields sometimes drove over my fence without even seeing it. One time that started a grass fire on the hill.

"Daisy got mastitis, an infection in the udder, and I had to treat her for it. Then she got cowpox, which is related to smallpox in humans; that gave her little scabs all over her skin. I didn't dehorn her when she was young because I thought she was going to be a beef cow. She grew big, dangerous horns, though, so I had the vet come and cut them off. Unlike antlers on deer, horns are living tissue. The vet used big nipper things—like you'd use to lop branches off a tree—and no anesthetic. I felt bad because afterward Daisy just stood there with a very bad headache and blood squirting from little arteries.

"I bred her again, and she had a bull calf, Matador. At some point, I ended up with seven cows and steers, all packed in a little barn not much bigger than a storage shed, although they spent most of their time in the pasture. After the episode with dehorning Daisy, I bought an electric dehorner, which was a lot less painful for the cows. When I dehorned the calves, I fed them milk afterward, and that was all it

Around fourteen months a cow will be ready to breed. Once she calves, her udder will fill with milk.

In one day, with a milking machine, a cow can produce ten to twelve gallons of milk a day. Even if it is turned into cheese and yogurt, this is more milk than one family needs.

took to make them happy again. The little nubs just popped off a couple days later.

"Eventually I got a milking machine from a farmer. He wasn't using it and just gave it to me. I started getting a lot more milk. We made cheese and butter, ice cream and yogurt. We fed some milk to the calves and pigs, but we threw out a lot of milk. One cow makes way more milk than a family can use, and it's illegal to sell it from home."

After four years, when Andy graduated from high school and went to college, he had to dispose of his herd. "I gave Daisy to a family who had just moved to the country. They wanted to get back to a simple lifestyle and live close to nature. They were interested in

The milking machine revolutionized the dairy industry. By hand, one dairyman might milk fifteen cows. With a milking machine, the same man could milk sixty. The first vacuum milking machine was patented in 1868, but fifty years passed before a practical machine became widely used. The basic milking machine consists of a vacuum pump, a stainless steel tank, and cups into which the cow's teats are inserted.

In the hand-milking days, a cow delivered four to five gallons of milk a day. Today, with improved genetics and with milking machines, cows can deliver ten to twelve gallons of milk daily.

producing their own milk and making cheese. Unfortunately, it was more work than they expected. She was too much for them to handle, so I ended up taking her back. I also had two young steers. I couldn't leave them for Mom to care for so I sold them all at the livestock market. Somebody bought the steers for 'feeders'—they would feed them until big enough to eat, then sell them for beef. I don't know what happened to Daisy. I hope someone put her in their dairy herd."

Andy's experience is just one example of what it's like to grow up on a farm. For other rural kids, the experience is quite different. Many times, life is like a spoiled child on Christmas morning: no matter what he gets, it's not what he thinks he wants. A child born in a rural area may long for bright lights and action, stores within walking distance, and a great paying job. Meanwhile, some urban kids might be

Small family-run farms were common about one hundred years ago. Today they are being replaced by large farms and development.

Gross domestic product (GDP) is defined as the total value of all goods and services produced within the country in a year. It includes everything: shoelaces, cars, cell phones, tattoos, videos, and farm products. No one actually counts everything produced. The number is an estimate.

attracted to the adventures of rural life, not to mention a real pet horse. The reality of either life seldom matches the vision. Growing up on the farm can be either better or worse than you can imagine. Along with the freedom to roam the woods and fields comes hard, smelly work and long, irregular hours.

One hundred years ago, most kids grew up on small farms. As the population grew and machines replaced manual labor, small farms began to disappear. People moved to the cities and suburbs looking for better paying jobs and an easier way of life. Today, less than 2 percent of the U.S. population lives on farms. In 2001, fewer than one million people lived on Canadian farms.

In 2004, 13,390 farms disappeared from the United States. Larger farms bought them out, or the landowners sold their property for housing developments, department stores, schools, and hospitals. In spite of this, agriculture remains the largest industry in the United States and the third–largest industry in Canada. Farm products account for 20 percent of the gross domestic product.

Improved farming techniques and highly efficient farm machinery make it possible for fewer people to produce more food on less land and in less time. Computer software now helps farmers find the perfect nutrient balance for his cow's feed, which then produces the

The idea of living on a farm appeals to many young people. Despite all the hard work, farm life offers the opportunity to live close to nature.

Farmer use special terms for cattle in their everyday speech that may not be familiar to others:

cow: a mature female

bull: a mature male

calf: a young cow or bull

heifer: a cow that has not borne a calf

steer: a castrated male

maximum quantity of high-grade milk. Massive, high-tech tractors plow thirty-six acres (14.6 hectares) per hour. Even though farmers have these modern tools at their disposal, however, such technology is still too expensive for many smaller or part-time operations. These people continue to farm the old way, with lots of hard physical labor.

For many people, the appeal of farm life is the opportunity to live close to nature. The soil, the trees, the plants, the animals, and even insects play an important role in the cycle of nature that provides food for all of us.

CHAPTER 2
Farm Animals

A couple times a year, Jason White and his family drive to the city to visit his in-laws. His mother-in-law really enjoys putting on a big family meal; she cooks like a professional chef. This particular evening, she set an elegant table, and they sat down to a porterhouse steak dinner. Jason brought the steaks because his brother raises beef cattle. You can't buy steaks like these in a store; they are so tender you can cut them with a spoon. Every year, Jason purchased a side of beef from him at wholesale prices.

The table conversation naturally turned to the main course.

"This is the best steak I ever ate!" exclaimed Bill, Jason's brother-in-law. Bill dined frequently at exclusive restaurants in the city.

"It sure is!" agreed his sister Debbie. "Juicy, tender, and totally delicious."

Jason was starting to feel he was in the middle of a television commercial for Pleasant Valley Farm Beef, but he wanted to contribute something to the conversation. "Walter was a great steer," he said between bites.

"Walter?" Jason's father-in-law's fork stopped halfway between his mouth and the plate.

"I met Walter once." Jason continued. "He loved music. When my son played his cornet, Walter came up to the edge of the pasture and bellowed right along."

Did you ever realize, one sentence too late, that you should have stopped while you were ahead? Silence replaced the usual tinkling and clinking of silverware on china.

"Delicious fruit salad!" exclaimed Jason's wife.

The Difference Between a Pet and a Product

Close association with many animals changes rural kids' perspectives on animals. Birth and death occur regularly, and living on a farm requires a different attitude toward animals, especially on farms engaged in the production of animals for food. Farm kids who raise their own steers or pigs naturally grow fond of their animals—but they are not pets. A 4-H club member raises a calf, feeds it, brushes it, and trains it to walk on a lead. She shows it at the fair and wins a blue ribbon. The calf sells at auction to a beef producer. Sometimes the line between "pet" and "product" blurs. It's a fact of life. Sooner or later, kids in 4-H have to face the inevitable and sell the animal to someone who ultimately produces sausage, bacon, steaks, and burgers.

Farm kids have a unique relationship with the animals that they raise. The animals may seem like pets, but eventually they must be sold for use as food.

One difficult reality of farm life is that cows must be separated from their calves shortly after birth. This helps make milking easier.

Adjusting to Country Life

Alesia, born in the city, met and fell in love with Vaughn, a country boy. She loves animals, but she quickly discovered some differences between pets and products. "That was a hard adjustment, selling off calves and realizing that we couldn't keep them. I made pets out of the first heifers and bull calves I ever raised after I married Vaughn. I named them, taught them how to lead. That was never done on this farm before. I groomed them every day. When they grew up, Vaughn tried to milk them, but he couldn't drive them into the *parlor*. They weren't used to being pushed. I went up ahead into the parlor and called them. They just walked right in after me!

Training to Lead

A lead is a rope or leash. Training to lead means teaching an animal to walk on a leash. A cow, steer, or horse that was trained to lead as a calf or colt is much easier to handle when full grown.

"If calves were born in the cold weather, I put them in the wheelbarrow and brought them into the house. We built a stall in the laundry room. One year, Vaughn bought me a little jersey calf for Valentine's Day. He hid it, but my daughter found it and thought Daddy had bought her a deer because it was brown. She and her father came into the house and placed it in my arms. It was such a pet we let it inside regularly, and I dressed it in rubber pants so it wouldn't mess up the house. Almost every time I let it in, though, somebody would show up to visit. They'd think we were backwoods hillbillies."

As much as Alesia still loves animals, she had to accept some harsh facts. Mother cows are separated from their calves shortly after birth.

"I never could understand why you would take the calves away from the mothers. I thought it was just horrible. These mothers bawl for their calves. I had a real issue with that. Vaughn tried to explain to me that it just wouldn't work to leave them together. You can't milk the cows if they're left with their calves—he said they get upset and won't stand still for their milking.

"I convinced him to let me try to make it work. I quickly learned that when the calves tried to follow their mother into the parlor, it created chaos. Cows were bawling, both the mothers and the others. It was awful. I learned that the longer they stayed together, the harder it was to separate them in the end."

Spring and New Births

Kids growing up on farms often learn different things than their urban counterparts. Lindsay's family, for example, keeps a few chickens and roosters, and Lindsay decided to sit on a **clutch** of eggs to see if they'd hatch.

"I wanted to prove to Mom that I could hatch chicks. She didn't believe me. I used to sit for hours on an egg or two wrapped in a cloth. One of our neighbors heard what I was doing. He lent me his incubator and I didn't tell Mom. She was pretty surprised when I came up with seven chicks, but she figured out pretty fast that I had help."

When Lindsay started breeding her chicks, she also learned about genetics. "I learned the hard way that you shouldn't make chicks from parents that are brothers and sisters. Two of the babies couldn't walk, and one was blind in one eye. Dad had to 'take care' of the lame chicks. I sat on the five remaining chicks in a nest made from a blanket curled up at the edges. The chicks ran in and out of the nest and under me. Then one day—one tragic day—I was sitting on them reading a book and discovered one suffocated under me. It was the one I had given to my sister Kayla. I screamed. It wasn't so much that a chick died but that I'd killed my sister's chick. Kayla was like, 'Whatever.' I tried to give her another one but she wouldn't take it until I started crying.

"Those human-raised chickens were so tame and **docile** we used them as props in plays. We'd sit the chickens down where we wanted them and they stayed. We'd tell them, 'Good chicken!'"

The Fertile Haystack

Spring is the season of new life on a farm. Elliot Gardner, raised on a farm, describes a busy spring day inside the straw stack.

In the spring, babies of all shapes and sizes arrive at the farm.

"While my folks lived on the Medberry farm, an unusual event occurred. The threshing machine blew the grain straw into the barnyard, creating a huge straw stack. When we turned the livestock into the barnyard, the animals would eat a hole into the side of the stack large enough so that smaller stock, such as sheep or pigs, could take shelter there.

"One rainy, cold spring morning, Giles, our hired hand, noticed a cow and calf at the entrance to a large straw stack hole. He and Dad went out into the rain to herd them into warmer quarters. While at this task, they noticed that just a bit further in the hole was a brood sow with a litter of pigs. Not only were the little pigs suffering from cold, but there were more of them than mama had places for at the

Many young people dream of owning a pet horse. However, very few actually realize how much work goes into caring for a horse.

table. Dad and Giles found a wooden box, threw in some straw, placed the little squealers on the straw, and carried them to the house. In the kitchen they placed the box on two chairs in front of the kitchen stove to warm the newcomers. Returning to the straw stack, Dad and Giles started to herd the old pig out of the haystack and into the barn. They pulled her out of the hole, and out of the stack walked a cat followed by four kittens. Dad thought surely the cat and kittens were the end of it, but Giles crawled on hands and knees to the far end of the hole just to make sure. When he backed out into daylight, he was shaking with laughter. 'Frank,' he said, 'There's a hen and a dozen or so baby chicks back at the end of that hole.'"

Equine Rescue

Newspapers often carry stories of animals rescued from squalid conditions—dogs lying in cages full of feces, dead and starving cats, and poultry all living and dying together in a rat-infested shack with people whose motives no one understands. These stories make the news. But most abused animals don't appear in newspapers. They result from good intentioned but ignorant people.

Courtney helps her mother rescue horses from bad conditions. According to Courtney, "A lot of the horses that we've taken in were owned by people who loved their horse but didn't know how to care for it. The three we now have are all rescue cases. Two are now beautiful, but one is still full of parasites and missing half her hair. Her owners didn't mean to starve her, but they kept her in a stall closed up in the barn. They kind of forgot they owned a horse and didn't feed her. By the time we got her, she was almost dead.

"A lot of people think it would be cool to have a horse. They get one without sufficient knowledge of horses. They don't realize how much work goes into care or how much a horse eats. Horses are expensive pets. People get tired of the constant work of feeding and cleaning out the stall. Meanwhile, the horse may be starving. It is totally at the owner's mercy.

"We just picked up another. He supposedly was purchased at a rescue place, but the so-called rescue place was just buying horses that looked thin, then turning around and selling them. This horse is *emaciated*. He would not have survived a lot longer. He's pretty scary looking right now. It takes a lot of time and money to bring a horse back to health."

Courtney's family does more than restore horses to health. They also try to educate those interested in purchasing a horse or other farm animals. "We have a lot of different animals, but the horses are the most popular on our farm. Visitors come who desperately want their own horse. When I describe the work involved, they usually change their minds. If they still want a horse, we tell them to take riding lessons for a year to learn how to handle a horse. While taking riding lessons, learn about horses from people who own them. Read everything you can find about them. Join a 4-H club that works with horses. See if your interest continues. Many kids want a horse. Their parents give them one, and it's exciting at first, but as life goes on, they get bored. The horse is still there, though, and still needs care.

"Many people who didn't grow up around animals don't know how to treat them. Some people who visit our farm, especially young children, throw rocks at the animals or chase them just for fun, not realizing the stress they cause the animals. One teenager found an empty feed sack and started scooping up chickens and putting them in the sack. Why do people act like that?

"In a lot of families, the parents end up taking care of the kids' pets for them. Not in our family. The rule here is if you have a pet, their needs come before yours. They eat before you. Your hunger will remind you they are probably hungry, too."

If you are interested in horses, joining a 4-H club or enrolling in riding lessons is a good way to gain experience and decide whether you could really handle owning one.

Farming usually involves animals—livestock for profit and pets for companionship. Town and city dwellers must limit their pets to animals that fit in a house or yard, but on a farm, the options expand to cows, horses, donkeys, pigs, ducks, geese, and chickens. Many farms have less common animals as well—ostriches, peacocks, emus, pheasants, buffalo, and deer. Chances are you can find a similar *eclectic* mix in any rural area in North America, limited only by the climate. And kids who grow up on a farm learn a lot from interacting with these animals.

CHAPTER 3
Wild and Feral Encounters

Feral means wild, but the word most often describes domesticated species that exist without human aid. Feral cats, dogs, and pigs live anywhere they can find enough food to survive. Feral honeybees swarm out of a beehive and move into a hollow tree. On the farm, feral animals can damage crops or livestock, or spread diseases to domestic animals. They can also benefit the farmer. Feral cats, for example, reduce the rodent population in a barn. Feral honeybee colonies improve crop pollination, and when hived, provide a honey crop.

Into the Eye of the Swarm

As James rode his bicycle toward his grandparents' house, the sun seemed to go dark. Large insects flew into his face and glasses. Skidding to a stop, he found himself surrounded by honeybees swarming in a cloud perhaps fifty feet (15 meters) in diameter. The swirling mass drifted along the road at about five miles per hour. They headed toward an apple tree, and within minutes, they settled into a cluster about the size of a football. The branch from which they hung drooped almost to the ground.

Honeybees start new colonies by swarming. In late spring, when *nectar* is plentiful, bees raise new queens. They build extra large queen cells in the comb. The queen lays eggs in the queen cells, and the workers feed the larvae a special enriched diet. Before new queens mature, the old queen and one-third to one-half of the bees leave the hive. They settle in a dense cluster anywhere in size from a grapefruit to a basketball, sometimes on a tree branch, sometimes on the bumper of a car. Scout bees search for a new home, and within two hours to two days, the entire swarm flies to the new home.

James learned to handle honeybees from his father, who kept a few colonies until he developed an allergy to bee stings. With the un-used equipment stored in the barn, James decided to capture the swarm. He rode back home, got an empty hive, and balanced it on his bicycle. Returning to the swarm, he placed the hive underneath. He knew a swarm was not inclined to sting, so he wore no veil or gloves. He jerked the branch from which the swarm hung. Most of the bees dropped into the hive, and he gently lowered the cover, giving the bees time to move away and avoid being crushed. Luckily, the queen fell into the hive and stayed inside. By evening, all the bees were inside. James and his mother brought the hive home after dark,

In the spring, some honeybees leave
their hives in search of a new one.
While a few scouts search for a good
hive location, the rest of the swarm
forms a dense cluster on a tree branch.

Honeybee quiz:

1. How many flowers must honeybees tap to make one pound of honey?

2. How far does a hive of bees fly to bring you one pound of honey?

3. How much honey does the average worker honeybee make in her lifetime?

4. How fast does a honeybee fly?

5. How much honey would it take to fuel a bee's flight around the world?

6. How many flowers does a honeybee visit during one collection trip?

Answers:

1. Two million.

2. Over 55,000 miles.

3. 1/12 teaspoon.

4. About 15 miles per hour.

5. About one ounce (or two tablespoons).

6. 50 to 100.

By wearing protective clothing and using a smoker, beekeepers minimize the chances of receiving a sting.

placing it behind the barn. That was the first colony he had caught by himself.

The first thing people think about keeping bees is the danger and pain of stinging. James describes his own experience: "When I first started working bees with my Dad, I never got stung, even when I didn't wear gloves. Like all beekeepers, we use a smoker—a metal can with a spout and bellows. You light a little fire in it and puff smoke into the hive. It calms the bees down. If you work on sunny days when the older bees are in the fields and move slowly, there is almost no danger of stings.

"The first time I got stung, I almost quit beekeeping. A bee got in my veil and stung me right under the eye. That hurt! Then Dad

Most barn cats lead a rough life. They compete for food, suffer from infections, and risk injury from farm equipment and other animals.

started swelling up when he got stung. He let the hives go, and one winter, they all died. But once I had my own hive, I learned a lot.

"For instance, different hives have different temperaments. Since I started beekeeping on my own, one of our neighbors gave me a 'hot' hive he wanted to get rid of. You'd practically just look at it, and they'd attack. It was also falling apart, so I had to take out the honeycomb and put it in a new hive. The bees came out at me and started climbing up my pant legs. After about the fifth sting, I was surprised they didn't seem to hurt as much anymore. By the time I was done, I felt a little light-headed. I probably got twenty or thirty stings. They don't bother me much anymore, unless I get stung on the lip or nose, somewhere where there are a lot of nerve endings. Most people, when they think of bee stings, actually remember the pain from a wasp or yellow jacket sting. Their stings hurt way more than a honeybee's."

Barn Cats

Every year animal shelters *euthanize* an estimated 15 million homeless cats and dogs. That doesn't include the animals abandoned and left to die by owners who for various reasons tire of the responsibility of pet ownership. These owners mistakenly believe their pet will either return to the wild or find their way into a friendly farmer's barn. More likely, tame animals unused to hunting will slowly starve to death. Farmers frequently find abandoned animals at their doorstep or barn. Their barn likely already has too many cats. The new arrival's fate will vary, depending on the farmer.

Most farmers do the best they can. For example, Dick never turns away an abandoned cat and accepts them from people who can no longer keep them. He has one requirement: "Never ask me what happened to your cat." A barn cat's life is nasty, brutish, and short. Dick provides milk for them, but they have to find their own meat. He cannot afford veterinary care or sterilization for thirty or forty cats.

Cows step on them. Tractor wheels roll over them. They suffer from parasites, diseases, and eye infections. Coyotes eat them. "They are not quite at the top of the food chain," Dick explains.

Cats abandoned at Green Haven Farm suffer a better fate. Growing up in the city, Alesia had enjoyed pet cats, while her husband Vaughn grew up thinking of cats as a necessary nuisance whose job was to keep down the rodent population. His family would never have considered letting a cat into the house. One winter, though, someone dropped off a female cat at Alesia and Vaughn's farm. Abandoned female cats are usually pregnant, and sure enough, shortly after her arrival, she gave birth. Because of the cold weather, Alesia insisted the cat and kittens come in the house. Mama cat prowled through the house looking for a secluded spot to nurse her kittens and finally found a hole in the upstairs bathroom wall. Inside the wall, a ledge dropped off to the first floor. Within hours, a kitten fell off, landing between the walls on the first floor, and crying piteously. "It was trapped and I freaked out!" said Alesia.

Vaughn's first reaction was: "It'll stop crying and eventually the smell will go away."

The mother cat was upset and crying. Alesia wanted to cut open the wall. She said, "Vaughn unscrewed the electric outlet, slid out the metal box, pulled out the kitten, and saved our marriage."

There were always too many cats on the farm when Vaughn was growing up. New arrivals more than compensated for the high mortality rate. Still the hardest-hearted pragmatist may have a soft spot.

Vaughn raised Holstein cattle—the mottled black and white breed—and one day, a mottled black and white kitten arrived, cold and hungry. Vaughn named him "Holstein." Mild-mannered and friendly, Holstein sat beside Vaughn as he milked. He arrived at every milking and stayed the whole time. Vaughn would never spend money on a barn cat; his philosophy was: If a cat is sick or dying, let nature take its course. One day, though, Holstein showed up limping on a swollen leg.

Vaughn took him to the vet.

Cats are necessary on a farm. They help keep the rodent population under control.

Rescuing Wild Animals

Agricultural land provides habitat for 75 percent of the nation's wildlife, so it's not unusual for someone growing up on a farm to cross paths with wild animals. In nearly every encounter, wild animals should be left alone. Young birds and mammals may look like orphans, but the mother frequently leaves a baby for long periods of time while she searches for food. Raccoons, woodchucks, or other mammals that act strangely may have rabies or other diseases. Sick or injured animals require the assistance of a trained wildlife rehabilitator.

Organizations such as barncats.org try to find homes for un-wanted cats. They first spay or neuter them, provide vaccinations, and then, for a small fee, the owner of a barn gets a cat—and the cat gets a home.

Brad has had some experience rescuing wild turkeys. "Wild turkeys first moved into this area five, maybe ten years ago. Farmers weren't used to them. The turkeys nest in hay fields, and during hay season, farmers would mow right over the nest, often killing the mother. Some farmers didn't worry about it, but most couldn't leave the eggs to the coyotes. They'd stop mowing right in the middle of the job, put the eggs in their hat, and bring them to me. They knew I raised a few chickens and had an incubator. There is some danger of spreading diseases between domestic birds and wild ones, al-though I've never had a problem. Over the years I raised four or five clutches of turkey eggs. I don't know if it was legal or not. I just couldn't see letting them die if I could help it.

"Sometimes I'd incubate them, but it's a lot of work taking care of the **poults**. I preferred sticking the eggs under a **broody** hen if I had one, and I usually did at that time of year. The mother hen took care of them for me.

"The problem with mixing two species like hens and turkeys is that the turkeys are more **precocious** than chicks. When turkeys are only about ten days old, they'll fly up into a tree to roost for the night. Mama Hen runs back and forth on the ground squawking at them, trying to coax them down to nestle under her wings.

"Wild turkeys don't ever seem to become quite tame. By the time they are nearly full size, they wander farther and farther afield. Then

Wild animals such as raccoons should be left alone. If they appear sick or injured, enlist the help of a trained wildlife rehabilitator.

Wild turkeys sometimes nest in hay fields. If a farmer mows over a turkey nest and kills the mother, the eggs or babies will not survive on their own.

one day they don't return. Well, there was one we had that was almost tame, named Bill. He was the firstborn of two eggs. We kept him warm in a cardboard box under a brooder lamp in the kitchen. The first night he just cried and cried. Every time I looked in, he stopped. Newborn birds *imprint* on the first thing they see that moves, and I guess Bill thought I was his mother. I couldn't sit and stare at him all night, so I got to thinking, 'Turkeys are smarter than most people think, but still they're not that bright.' I found as large a picture of a human as I could find—the head of Perry Como on an old record cover. I leaned it against the wall of the box, and Bill quieted right down. The next day his sister hatched, and we had no more trouble. But as they grew, Bill was the friendliest turkey I ever met. He and Claudia liked to go walking with us all over the farm. We humans were part of the flock. They spread out about fifty feet away and walked parallel to us."

The Dear Dead Robin

One spring, when there was more than the usual amount of spring work to be done on the Medberry farm, Elliot's father hired an extra man to help catch up with the spring plowing and planting. This guy was a rough customer with little or no feeling for man or beast. One day when he was plowing near the house, Elliot wandered out to watch. Robins were working the freshly plowed ground, picking up worms, and just enjoying themselves in the spring sunshine. Suddenly the man picked up a rock and let it fly at the robins in the *furrow* behind him.

All the birds escaped but one. Elliot, who was just a little guy at the time, wanted to do something nice for the poor dead bird. He carefully picked up the robin and started for the house, with no real plan in mind at all.

Inside, he took the feathery little body into the parlor, a room that was kept nice for company. Most of the time, no one went in there except to clean and dust. Elliot sat in a chair, rested the dead robin on his lap, and looked at it. He was gripped with the conviction that he must do something for this poor thing that had been snuffed out in the prime of life.

As he looked around the parlor, his eyes came to rest on his mother's tall glass vase, a wedding present his mother thought the world of. Suddenly, it seemed to Elliot that the kindest thing he could do was to use the vase as a last resting place for the dead robin. He got to his feet and gently placed the robin in the flared top of the vase.

The robin seemed to nestle in nicely. "It was rather like a glass nest," Elliot remembered years later. "If one did not look closely at

Baby birds will often be left alone while the mother searches for food. This does not mean that they are abandoned.

the closed eyes and lopping head, it seemed quite lifelike. I had a good feeling about this act of kindness and quietly left the room.

"For the next few days, I would peek in the parlor door each morning and view the remains. All was well. My heart felt easy in my chest. But then, of course, there came a day. . . .

"One noontime Father came to the house for dinner and said to my mother, 'Freda, I smell something in this house. Do you suppose there is a dead rat down cellar?'

"'I don't know,' my mother replied, 'but perhaps you should take a look.'

"But there was no dead rat in the cellar or anywhere else. By the next morning, the unpleasant aroma filled the entire house, and Mother started on a search, following her nose. Of course, she found my poor, mortified robin at rest in her prized vase.

"Now my mother liked birds—but not in the condition in which she found this one. The worst of it was that she knew instantly just how the robin had found its way to its resting place. I nearly got a spanking for my act of kindness. I was let off on the promise that it would never happen again. It never did."

CHAPTER 4
Country Life Meets City Life

Lauren's dad puts his hay into large round bales, about five feet (1.5 meters) in diameter. He then wraps each bale in heavy white plastic to protect it from rain and preserve the hay's nutritional value. When Lauren's younger cousins came from the city to visit and saw the big white bales lined up along the edge of the field, they asked, "What are those?"

"Giant marshmallows!" Lauren said. "They grow like mushrooms out here."

"No way!"

"Where do you think marshmallows come from? You city folk! You never realized that everything has to grow somewhere."

Her cousins gazed with awe at the giant white shapes. "Can you eat them?"

"We do all the time."

"Can I try one?"

"Sure. Go take a bite." The children ran into the field before Lauren could stop them. Each took a large bite off the corner of a bale.

"Yuck!" They turned accusing eyes on Lauren.

She tried to explain that the marshmallows just weren't ripe yet, but her cousins figured out the joke. Luckily, they had a sense of humor.

The Blending of Town and Country Lifestyles

Town life and country life used to be very different. Country kids worked on the farm, while town kids spent most of their time in houses and stores or walking along streets. Until the late 1930s, students in the country attended one-room schoolhouses, while town kids attended larger schools. Many folks in their seventies and eighties remember those days.

Seventy-three-year-old Gary likes to reminisce about his experience in a one-room schoolhouse. He rose from a first-grader speaking broken English mixed with German to *valedictorian* of the sixth-grade class. "Of course," he adds, "I was the only sixth-grader in the school."

School *centralization* brought together children from diverse backgrounds. Now, many students from the country rode the school bus to town and attended the same schools as town kids. At the same time, farm mechanization—the use of ever-bigger machinery on farms—freed farm children from some of the long hours they used to spend working on the farm. They could more easily participate

In the past, rural students attended a one-room schoolhouse when they weren't too busy helping out on the farm.

People who live in the city may have some misconceptions about what life is like on a farm.

Lauren's cousin was partly right about eggs coming from factories. Some egg producers pack chickens into small cages with a sloped floor. Food comes by a conveyor system. Manure drops through the mesh floor. The eggs roll out of the sloped cage, onto a conveyor belt, and into the processing facility. All the conditions are controlled for optimum egg production.

with their town friends on school-sponsored athletic teams and other activities.

Despite the merging of town and country lifestyles, old *stereotypes* remain. Alesia, who grew up in the city and moved to the country when she married, recalls a visit from relatives:

"When my family came up from Philadelphia, they had odd notions about farm life. For instance, they thought we did not have indoor plumbing and used an outhouse. And they thought we gathered all our hay with pitchforks, cooked over an open fire, and slept in the haymow. They knew milk came from cows, but they hadn't thought much about where the milk actually left the cows' bodies. When they saw the actual milking process, they wanted no part of it. We had some fun with them, telling them skim milk came from thin cows and chocolate milk came from Brown Swiss cows. They were glad to get back to civilization."

When Lauren invited her Baltimore cousin to gather eggs from the chicken coop with her, she ran into another example of city ignorance. "We asked her if she'd like to collect eggs from the chickens," Lauren remembers.

But her cousin said, "You can't collect the eggs! They come from factories."

"No, they don't." Lauren showed her the nesting boxes in the chicken coop. Reaching under a hen, she pulled out two eggs. "My cousin thought it was so gross! She thought chickens 'pooped' eggs."

"Free range" chickens live a more normal life, at least for a chicken. Rather than being crowded into a cage, they wander in and out of their chicken coop and can scratch in the dirt, looking for bugs.

Playing Chicken

When Garret was looking to make some extra money, his parents suggested he go into the egg business. People pay more for "free range" chicken eggs, and he could set up an egg stand in their front yard.

"We already had a few chickens. Then Mom and Dad bought me twenty-five more *pullets*. One day Dad was inside, talking on the phone, when he saw a big dog run past the window. Dad ran out in his socks, calling me on the way. We chased the dog away, but he injured or killed twenty chickens, so we had to butcher them right away.

"After Dad chopped their heads off, he hung them on the clothesline to drip. It was an awful sight, that row of headless chickens. You've heard the expression, 'running around like chickens with their heads cut off'? Well, it's true. Dead chickens run and flop for a while, but they're feeling no pain. I had to catch the headless chickens that flapped themselves right off the clothesline.

"Just at that moment, some people from town came to buy eggs. They were back-to-nature, animal-rights people, and that's why they liked our eggs. So when they drove up and saw all those headless chickens flapping and dripping in the wind, their mouths just hung open. At that instant, I came around the corner holding another wounded chicken by its feet. Dad stood at the chopping block in a

Many eggs at the grocery store come from chickens that live their lives at an egg packaging facility. Chickens raised on small farms live a more normal life.

Country kids and city kids are not so far apart today, thanks to television and the Internet.

bloodstained apron, a big dripping knife in his hand. Those people haven't been back to buy more eggs."

City people may sometimes make fun of "country hicks," but country kids think "city folk" can be pretty silly. However, the media helps to bring the two perspectives closer together. For instance, the introduction of television brought town and country kids even closer together, as they shared the common experience of watching the same programs. By the time town kids had access to many channels on cable, the farm kids could watch by satellite dish. Now kids in the city could watch television shows about people living in the country—and meanwhile, the country kids were learning plenty about city life from watching television.

As technology evolved, country folks managed to keep up with townspeople, despite problems associated with distance from services. Today, 52 percent of rural residents use the Internet, only slightly less than the 66 percent of urban and suburban users. The Internet is bringing people from opposite sides of the globe closer together—and it is also helping to span the distance between farm and city.

CHAPTER 5
Farm Machines

"**Farmer** job" or "farmer fix" is a *derogatory* term for a bad repair on machinery. When a big machine breaks down, it's usually in the middle of a big job. The baler quits just before a thunderstorm strikes, threatening to ruin the hay crop. A wheel bearing on the manure spreader seizes up in the middle of the field because manure corroded the metal. There's no time to get the machine to the repair shop. A new part has to be ordered, but for the cost of some repairs, a farmer can almost buy a secondhand machine. So most often he "makes do" with baling wire, duct tape, a hammer, or his own welder.

If a farmer had to pick all her apples by hand, it would be long, tiring work. Instead, farmers use machines to help speed up the process.

Running an Apple Harvester

The year Bill turned eighteen, his neighbor, an *orchardist*, bought a used hydraulic apple shaker for harvesting sauce apples. It would really speed up production. Mr. Schmidt asked Bill if he'd like to help run it.

"It's got an engine, wheels, and levers? Sure!" Bill thought it would be similar to a video game.

Monday morning at 7:00, Bill got his first lesson. The harvester consisted of two separate mirror-image machines, each with its own engine and steering wheel. Bill and Mr. Schmidt worked together, one on each side of an apple tree. Pushed together, the machines encircled the tree. Each had its own steel arm with a claw at the end. With a row of levers, the operator extended the arm into the tree, and a large metal claw grasped a limb. With the flick of another switch, the arm vibrated the entire limb, knocking the apples off the branch. They fell onto a conveyor and rolled into a wooden bin. Bill and Mr. Schmidt climbed into the seats, started the engines, and rolled the machine toward the orchard.

Once the apple harvest commences, there is intense pressure to work swiftly. Apples must be harvested during a narrow span of time. Harvesting too early or too late can cost thousands of dollars in reduced crop value. Mr. Schmidt had at least a half dozen apple varieties, and they were harvested in the order in which they ripened: Macintosh, followed by Cortlands, Ida Reds, Red Delicious, Romes, and finally Northern Spys.

They reached the orchard and closed the machines around the first tree. Bill grabbed a limb and shook it. "This could be fun," he muttered to himself. The novelty wore off by late morning, though, and in the early afternoon, Mr. Schmidt's hydraulic arm broke right off at the shoulder.

Mr. Schmidt noted that the half-inch thick steel plate had been welded at that spot before. He walked back to the barn and returned with a tractor towing a huge old welder. He showed Bill a crank. "You crank start the welder engine. As soon as it kicks, the crank pulls loose, right in your hand. Go ahead and start it."

Bill cranked, and the welder fired, but the crank stuck to the engine shaft, spinning at an incredible speed, ready to fly off and kill someone at any second. Mr. Schmidt dove toward the machine and hit the "off" switch. The crank dropped harmlessly to the ground. Mr. Schmidt didn't say anything, but this time he started the welder himself. Half an hour later, they continued harvesting.

At 7:00 that evening, they shut down the machines, and Bill staggered home. Back to work at 7:00 the next morning, they started where they left off the day before. Mr. Schmidt's harvesting arm broke off again. He sent Bill for the tractor and welder. Four times the arm broke; and four times Mr. Schmidt welded it back, muttering under his breath each time.

Sometimes the hydraulic arms couldn't get a good grip on a limb because of its angle. When that happened, Mr. Schmidt sent Bill into the tree to manually shake the branches. Sometimes Bill shook all the branches while Mr. Schmidt welded. By evening, they had barely completed two rows.

"It doesn't make sense," Mr. Schmidt growled at Bill. "That arm shouldn't be busting off like that." Bill didn't dare suggest perhaps Mr. Schmidt was too rough on his arm.

The third day, Mr. Schmidt grinned like the Cheshire cat. "I talked to a **metallurgist** last night. He told me what's wrong. Repeated welding makes the metal brittle."

Bill wheeled the **oxyacetylene torch** into the orchard, and Mr. Schmidt turned it up high and heated the steel white hot. He held it at the heat for five or ten minutes, then welded the arm—for the last time. This time it held.

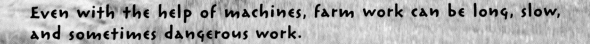

Even with the help of machines, farm work can be long, slow, and sometimes dangerous work.

Up and down the rows, they moved the machines. At night, they moved apple bins out of the orchard with forklifts and loaded them onto a tractor-trailer.

"See that underpass?" Mr. Schmidt asked Bill. The road at the end of the orchard ran under the state highway. "I saw somebody parked down at the end of our orchard, stealing our apples. I jumped in the truck and took off after them. Problem is the truck doesn't fit through that underpass. I forgot. Took the whole top row of apples off the truck." He laughed at himself.

Some of the orchards were planted on steep hills. None of Mr. Schmidt's farm vehicles had brakes. Bill learned to "double clutch" into first gear to slow down.

They finished harvesting in mid-November. Bill, grateful to still be alive, applied to college. He decided to major in accounting.

Repairing an old tractor may require some effort, but in the end it will be worth all the hard work.

Repairing and Operating Old Equipment

When Andy moved to the farm as a teenager, he found a variety of rusty farm implements of various ages and the Farmall tractor. Andy decided to put in a crop.

"That first year I put in wheat. I tried to use the old plow, but it didn't work worth beans. Finally, a neighbor said, 'You've got to put new points on that thing. That might help out.' I went to the farm supply store and bought plow points, put them on, and by golly, that thing would plow and turn over the dirt just slick. I planted wheat in an old hay field, which isn't a good idea because the hayseeds germinate and compete with the wheat. It was a bad wheat year, and I ended up with about half a truckload of wheat.

"I was working for Joe Judd that summer, and he **combined** the wheat for me and charged me a week's pay. That was probably more than fair, but he didn't tell me until payday.

"The next year I decided to plant ten acres (4 hectares) of corn. I probably made some money on the corn. Judd planted it for me, since I didn't have a planter. Once the corn comes up, it needs cultivating. You drive the tractor with the tires between the rows and the cultivator breaks up the soil and kills the weeds. I thought I could make my own cultivator out of scrap iron and my new welder. It took so long to make that the corn was too high for it to work. A neighbor let me use his corn picker, wagon, and **elevator** for the harvest. I fixed up the old **corncrib** at my grandmother's house, patching the walls and putting in new floorboards. Later that winter, we shelled and sold the corn. I don't remember how much money I made, but I did actually make a profit.

"I planted one field with Birdsfoot—a **legume** used for hay—and it came up almost pure. It was worth $300 a bushel then if you could get it certified. I hoped it would help pay for college. Ha ha. That didn't work out, but it made great hay.

Before the use of machines, farmers had to spend hundreds of hours to complete what can now be accomplished in only a few.

"When we cut hay for the cows we used an old horse-drawn hay rake, pulled by the tractor. My brother rode the rake, and I drove. Sometimes we'd switch. The rake pulled the hay into piles. When we came back with the wagon, instead of asking the neighbors for help, we pitched the hay on with forks like in the old days. Why did we do that? I guess I just wanted to say we did it ourselves."

When most people think of farms, they think of animals, nature, the simple life—forgetting that farmers depend on a variety of machines for their livelihoods. Two hundred years ago, these machines didn't exist, and in 1830, about 250 to 300 labor-hours were required to produce 100 bushels of wheat. Between 1850 and 1870, though, an

Antique Tractors: Rebuild or Restore?

They built old tractors to last. In spite of all the improvements in newer models, farmers still use fifty- to sixty-year-old tractors. Some like buying old tractors to rebuild or restore. Rebuilding involves putting a tractor back into working condition. Restoration involves returning the tractor to its original condition by finding original parts to replace broken ones. In both cases, the tractors are taken apart, cleaned, and repaired, then reassembled and painted. Antique tractors are a popular part of parades in small towns across North America.

expanded market for farm products spurred farmers to look for improved technology to increase their farms' production. As a result, by 1890, only forty to fifty labor-hours produced 100 bushels of wheat. In the 1890s, agriculture became increasingly mechanized and *commercialized*, and the trend just kept going. By 1987, only three labor-hours produced 100 bushels of wheat. As the twentieth century drew to a close, information technology and precision techniques were increasingly used in agriculture. But those old tractors were still chugging along.

Farm Machinery Timeline

18th Century	Oxen and horses are used to pull crude wooden plows; all sowing is done by hand, cultivating by hoe, hay and grain cutting with sickle, and threshing with a flail.
1790s	Cradle and scythe are introduced; cotton gin is invented.
1797	Charles Newbold patents first cast-iron plow.
1819	Jethro Wood patents iron plow with interchangeable parts
1834	McCormick reaper is patented; John Lane manufactures plows faced with steel saw blades.
1837	John Deere and Leonard Andrus begin manufacturing steel plows; practical threshing machine is patented.
1840s	Factory-made agricultural machinery increases farmers' need for cash and encourages commercial farming.
1841	Practical grain drill is patented.
1842	First grain elevator is built in Buffalo, New York.
1844	Practical mowing machine is patented.
1856	Two-horse straddle-row cultivator is patented.
1862–75	Change from hand power to horses characterizes the first American agricultural revolution.
1868	Steam tractors are tried out.

1880	William Deering puts 3,000 twine binders on the market.
1884–90	Horse-drawn combine is used in Pacific Coast wheat-growing areas.
1892	The first gasoline tractor is built by John Froelich.
1910–15	Big open-geared gas tractors are introduced in areas of extensive farming.
1915–20	Enclosed gears are developed for tractors.
1918	A small prairie-type combine with auxiliary engine is introduced.
1920–40	Farm production gradually grows due to the expanded use of mechanized power.
1926	A successful light tractor is developed.
1930s	All-purpose, rubber-tired tractor with complementary machinery becomes popular.
1942	Spindle cottonpicker is produced commercially.
1945–70	Change from horses to tractors and increasing technological practices characterize the second American agricultural revolution; productivity per acre begins sharp rise.
1954	Number of tractors on farms exceeds the number of horses and mules for the first time.
1959	Mechanical tomato harvester is developed.
1994	Farmers begin using satellite technology to track and plan their farming practices.

CHAPTER 6
Farm Safety

Andy describes one of several close calls with farm machinery: "I was working on a neighbor's farm chopping corn. A full wagon weighs between twelve and fifteen tons. As I pulled a loaded wagon down the driveway, I heard a 'clunk.' Looking back over my shoulder I saw the wagon wasn't where it was supposed to be. The wagon tongue had broken off the wagon, and now the tongue, still attached to the tractor, dragged on the ground—and fifteen tons of corn *silage* were coasting toward me. I was sitting on a tractor with no fenders, roll bar, or anything. If I accelerated and pulled out of the way, the wagon would take its own course, either hitting my neighbor's gas pumps—or veering the other way

Farming is dangerous work, especially for young people. Accidents often happen when children begin operating farm machinery before they are old enough.

and hitting the house. The other option was to apply the brakes and hope for the best. The tractor had one brake for each rear tire, and you operate both with one foot. Each required a different amount of force for equal stopping power. If one brake locked up and the other didn't, the tractor would pivot on the locked wheel, and the wagon would probably push the tractor over. I'd be dead.

"All this went through my mind in a split second. I pulled hard on the steering wheel, and pushed my foot sideways against both brake pedals, tipped just at the right angle to lock both wheels equally. I put all I had into those brakes. The wagon rammed into the tractor, and the wheels locked and skidded twenty feet before finally stopping."

Overloaded

Time is always short on a farm, and money is always tight. To compensate, a farmer may push equipment up to and sometimes beyond its limits. Andy pulled a large manure spreader with a small tractor. That's not a problem unless you are driving uphill.

"I was pulling an overloaded **tandem axle** spreader. Things went fine until I started up a hill. The tractor started chugging and I had to shift down. You have to stop a tractor to shift gears. The brakes wouldn't hold the tractor on the hill, so the trick is to wait just until it stops rolling forward, then quickly jam the shift lever into low and pop the clutch before you start coasting backward.

"I held on an instant too long. The tractor stalled and began coasting just as I shifted into neutral. Now I couldn't put it in gear, and it didn't have brakes to hold me on the hill. The wagon jackknifed one way. I spun the wheel to straighten it and jacked it the other way. I spun the wheel again, and it jackknifed the other way, all the while rolling backward down the hill. Letting it go would probably flip the tractor. Jamming it into gear would tear up the transmission or pop the front end up in the air, and could have rolled the tractor. You don't want to hurt the equipment. There's a lot of money in equipment—that's drilled into you when you're young. I made it to the bottom of the hill.

"My boss watched the whole thing. He commented, 'Now that was some fancy steering on that tractor!'"

Farming is the second–most dangerous industry, ranked just behind mining. According to the national safety council, in 2002, there were 730 agricultural-related deaths and almost 150,000 injuries. About 100 teenagers, age nineteen or younger, die each year on farms in the United States. On family farms, children too young to drive a car may operate large machinery. Inexperience, diverse conditions, and poorly maintained equipment lead to a high accident rate for youth.

Six Ways to Injure or Kill Yourself While Hitching an Implement to a Tractor

A Pennsylvania State University pamphlet, <u>Children and Safety on the Farm</u>, suggests potential hazards associated with various tasks often performed by young people on the farm. For example, when hitching or unhitching a farm implement from a tractor:

1. Implement could roll when the tongue is lifted, causing a crushing injury.

2. A heavy tongue may cause back strain when lifted.

3. If tractor operator miscalculates and does not stop in time when backing up to the wagon, helper may be crushed or run over by the rear tractor tire.

4. Attaching an implement to the tractor may result in crushing injuries to the hands or body.

5. Helper may be run over by the tractor or implement.

6. Helper may suffer a crushing injury to the feet if the implement tongue slips off the tractor drawbar.

Employers often don't take time to teach proper equipment operation, or they assume a young person can "learn it on the fly." Almost 80 percent of accidents involve tractor rollovers or passengers falling off.

Farm-related accidents aren't restricted to the United States. In Saskatchewan alone between 1990 and 1996, one in five farm accidents involved someone age nineteen or younger.

Driving over fields that are near a pond can be risky. If the ground is too soft, the tractor can end up stuck.

The Rut Season

Driving over soft or boggy ground can add many frustrating hours to a simple job. Andy had to learn his own tractor's limit the hard way.

"I was driving the tractor along the pond on soft ground, when the big rear wheels sank in the mud almost up to the axles. I borrowed the neighbor's tractor, although I don't know why he loaned it to a kid. He probably felt sorry for me. My older brother and I hooked a log chain to the two drawbars of each tractor, back to back. My brother started to pull as I spun our tractor's wheels in reverse. The neighbor's tractor's wheels dug their own ruts in the soft ground. Just as we pulled the stuck tractor out, the second one sank in up to its axles. We carefully pulled around and rehooked up the log chains. Just as we pulled the second tractor out, the first sank in again. It took all afternoon plus a lot of old lumber and stones shoved under the tires, but we finally got both tractors onto firm ground. I stayed out of the area after that."

Dangerous Animals

Machinery isn't the only danger on farms. Farm animals sometimes act unpredictably. Horses and cows unintentionally cause injury just because of their size. When Alesia first moved to the farm, she learned that not all cows are gentle:

"I went out to check on a cow that was calving in the pasture. She was fine. When I turned to leave, I noticed the herd had come up behind me. They were all staring, but one came up to the front of the herd looking strangely intent. *Why is she looking at me like that?* I thought. It was one of the heifers I raised and made into a pet—but she pawed the ground, tossed her head, and made odd woofing noises. Her eyes rolled back in her head, and I thought, *Oh my goodness, I'm about to die!* She charged me. I knew I had to scare her before she reached me.

"She ran full bore toward me. I ran at her screaming, yelling, and waving my arms. She jumped away and I started running toward the fence. I could hear her right behind me, catching up, so I swerved, ran at her again, and threw rocks. Each time she startled less and less. Finally, I thought to call for my dog. He came and challenged the heifer, allowing me to get closer to the fence. Then she circled around the dog and ran for me. There was one big round bale at the end of the pasture right between me and the fence line. I dove on one side of the bale and shot under the wire. The cow was right behind me. That cow tried to kill me! I had no idea that cows could be so aggressive."

4-H Tractor Certification

To address safety issues of teens operating tractors, all youth ages thirteen to fifteen who want to be hired to drive a tractor and other farm equipment must pass a course to legally operate the equipment. Those sixteen and older should attend but aren't required. Details vary from state to state, but safety is the major emphasis. The course also covers instruments and controls, maintenance, starting and stopping tractors, hitches, PTO and hydraulic systems, tractors and implements. Call your county cooperative extension for details.

Lindsay's Little Lamb

> Mary had a little lamb,
> Its fleece was white as snow.
> And everywhere that Mary went,
> The lamb was sure to go.

But,

> Lindsay had a little lamb,
> Its head as hard as a hammer.
> And everywhere that Lindsay ran,
> The lamb would try to ram her.

Lindsay's parents had surprised her on her birthday with a pet lamb. She bottle-fed it, brushed its coat, and cleaned up after it. Just like Mary's nursery rhyme lamb, it followed Lindsay everywhere. Bottle-feeding any mammal is a lot of work, but a bottle-fed animal bonds with its caregiver like an infant with its mother—usually.

One day, Lindsay's lamb, now nearly full grown, charged and rammed her, knocking her down. Her mother caught the sheep and led her to her stall, wondering out loud, "Is this the lamb that played volleyball with the children and performed in the church play?"

Female animals can become irritable and unpredictable when "in heat" (ready to mate). Two weeks after the incident, when the sheep's behavior should have returned to normal, the family had to find out. Lindsay stood in the driveway beside a deep snow-drift. If the sheep tried to charge, her mother could hold on, and if she slipped, Lindsay had the choice of leaping into the deep snow or rolling up in a ball. Her mother brought the sheep out of its stall. Kayla, Lindsay's older sister, watched the test from a safe distance. The sheep behaved docilely until it noticed Kayla. In an instant its eyes went red, its ears dropped back, and it charged like a ram. Mother lost her grip. Kayla screamed and leaped over a deep snowbank toward the house. The sheep jumped over the bank and nearly reached Kayla before her mother caught up and tackled it.

The sheep's behavior remains a mystery. Lindsay's parents called all the sheep experts they could locate. No one offered an explanation. The family loved their sheep, but it had to go. They sold it to a sheep dealer, warning him not to sell it to a family with children.

Horse Feet

Most horses are gentle, but they can injure a person accidentally by stepping on someone's foot or suddenly rearing up or fleeing when startled. A few horses are bad tempered.

When Taylor was showing a hard-to-handle horse to one prospective buyer, Taylor's three-year-old daughter ran up behind the horse. The horse kicked his hind feet up at her, and the hooves grazed her head, knocking her down. If he had made direct contact, she could have been severely injured or killed. "I lost a sale that day," Taylor explained, "But the next buyer got him cheap."

Horse accidents aren't always the horse's fault. Most accidents result from carelessness or inexperience of the handler.

"Hey, Lindsay, come on over here and climb on this horse," Kayla suggested to her eight-year-old sister. Kayla stood in the horse stall holding Peach, a strong-willed but good-natured miniature horse. Lindsay had no experience with horses, although Peach was just her size.

"No way. You think I want to get killed?"

"You won't get killed. I'll hold her head," Kayla assured her. "You can just sit on her." Lindsay always wanted to ride a horse. It looked easy. Maybe if she just sat on her. . . .

Lindsay describes what happened next: "I climbed up on the rail and put a leg over Peach's back. The stall door was open. You could see out the barn into the pasture. Then Kayla let go."

"I did not let go," Kayla interrupted. "Peach jerked her head out of my grip. Then she headed out of the barn at full speed."

"I was never on a horse before. I didn't even know to say 'whoa!' There wasn't any saddle or bridle. I just held on with all my might with my eyes closed, screaming. Peach shot around the pasture like she thought a bobcat was clawing at her back. Then, I think I jumped off."

"You fell off—backward," Kayla corrected.

"Right into a manure pile, which was better than a rock pile. And Kayla just laughed and laughed at me. I scraped up my arm pretty bad, but I could have been killed."

"It really was an accident," Kayla said.

"If you want to grow up on a farm," Lindsay added, "Better not have an older sister."

CHAPTER 7
A Career in Agriculture

At fourteen, Greg decided to restore his grandfather's abandoned apple orchard. He found information on pruning from the county cooperative extension office. He discussed his project with great uncle Alex, who had a degree in pomology (the science of fruit cultivation). After school and on weekends, he worked his way from one end of the orchard to the other, trimming water sprouts (fast-growing vertical branches that waste the tree's energy) and opening up the center of the trees to sunlight.

His first crop was disappointing, but Greg knew it took several years to restore old trees to a productive state. He took some apples to his uncle, who identified most of the varieties.

81

"You've got Baldwins, Twenty Ounce, Winter Bananas, and Wealthies here—old varieties you won't find in a supermarket anymore."

"Are all old varieties supposed to be shrunken and lopsided?"

"No, that's a pollination problem. There aren't enough native pollinating insects. You'll have to put some honeybee colonies in your orchard."

A small industry compared to other branches of agriculture, apiculture (beekeeping) is like the little rudder that turns a giant ship. Most people think honey is the primary product of the hive. In fact, pollination of farm crops is a far greater value. In the United States, the value of the increased crop yield by honeybee pollination is approximately 14.6 billion dollars. With an estimated 2.9 million colonies in the United States today, that means every honeybee colony adds over $5,000 in food value to the economy. According to the National Honey Board, "One out of every three bites of food consumed in the United States comes from crops pollinated by honey bees."

Greg's introduction to the importance of honeybees led him onto a different career path. By his seventeenth birthday, he was managing over forty honeybee colonies. He is now looking at agriculture colleges that teach apiculture. He has a lot of excellent choices, thanks to . . . Abraham Lincoln?

The quality of today's agricultural colleges and the vitality of American agriculture come in great part from Lincoln's foresight. His Homestead Act of 1862 offered free land to anyone willing to settle and farm it. That started the great westward movement of new settlers. Unfortunately, many settlers had little experience with agriculture. Foreseeing that problem, Lincoln also signed another act establishing land grant colleges in every state to teach agriculture and home economics. Until the establishment of the land grant colleges, all higher learning in the United States came from private colleges and universities at a cost too expensive for average citizens.

Apple trees depend on honeybees to pollinate their flowers. Without healthy pollination in the spring, there will be no apple crop in the fall.

Today, every state has a land grant university funded by county, state, and federal taxes. These universities have three responsibilities:

1. College-level education for students interested in agriculture.

2. Agricultural research such as developing new plant varieties, disease management, and more efficient farming practices.

3. Extension (education "extending" to the general public) provides free or low-cost information on a wide variety of agricultural and related subjects. Before computers, information

Abraham Lincoln signed an act requiring every state to establish a land grant college that would teach agriculture and home economics.

came from publications offered by colleges and available at the local cooperative extension offices. Extension also offers classes on many subjects. Now much of the same material can be acquired online.

The 4-H Program

One of the most successful offshoots of extension is the 4-H program.

At the turn of the twentieth century, agricultural researchers were frustrated. They developed new technologies to improve farming,

What are the 4 Hs?

My Head to clearer thinking

My Heart to greater loyalty

My Hands to larger service, and

My Health to better living

For my club, my community, my country and my world.

but farmers did not accept newfangled ideas easily. Young people, willing to try new ideas, accepted them much more quickly. When an idea worked, their parents could see it for themselves. They in turn accepted the new idea.

Educators realized that *progressive* ideas spread best through young people. Agriculture teachers organized clubs that stressed practical learning. These eventually became 4-H clubs. Today over seven million kids and teens belong to 4-H clubs just in the United States, and 4-H has also spread to sixty other countries.

While originally for rural youth, most members today live in cities and suburbs, and 4-H's mission has expanded to include character development, leadership training, and community service. Individual 4-H groups reflect the interest of their members. Rural clubs still focus on rural themes such as raising livestock, horseback riding, gardening, or food preservation. If you grew up on a farm, chances are you participated in one or more 4-H clubs. They remain one of the best sources of information and education for young people interested in agriculture. Every county in the United States has a cooperative extension office with information on local clubs, plus information on forming your own club.

For teens considering a career in agriculture, the next step may be looking at land grant colleges, either in your own state or another. Once again, the local cooperative extension office offers that information or you can find it on the Web. Colleges with two- and four-year programs are listed at www.hoards.com.

The Future of Farming

When most people think of agriculture, they visualize a stereotype: a man or woman wearing jeans, a flannel shirt, and a cap. He or she sits on a big tractor in an air-conditioned cab planting or chopping corn. Or perhaps he or she is gathering eggs or milking cows.

In truth, though, the diversity of options in agriculture is surprising, with over two hundred different jobs in areas such as *horticulture*, animal sciences, farming, business and economics, communication, and food sciences. Besides farming, agricultural careers include mechanic, meat inspector, veterinarian, *surveyor*, plant *geneticist*, dairy scientist, crop production adviser, and educator.

As the industry grows and changes, so does the need for skilled people. In the United States, a recently completed study showed that the number of job openings in the food and agricultural sciences exceeded the number of qualified graduates every year from 2000 through 2005.

Sideline and Hobby Farming

Full-time farming or other agricultural careers require a large investment in time and money. Fortunately, the farming lifestyle is

4-H clubs were formed as a way to introduce new technologies to farmers through their children.

also within reach of anyone inclined toward other occupations. Many people choose to live in the country and farm part time while commuting to a full-time job.

People interested in any aspect of agriculture now have the information available as close as their computer screens. Want to raise tomatoes in a pot on the patio? Raise trout? Show your calf at the county fair? Build a greenhouse? The information from various co-operative extension Web sites takes minutes to locate on the Internet. Even as fewer of North Americans farm for a living, membership in Future Farmers of America (now the National FFA Organization) has hit a twenty-two-year high. The number of farmers' markets across the country has doubled—and then some—since 1994. The more urban and suburban we become, the more farm life seems to fascinate us.

As people have moved away from farms and into high-tech careers, there often remains the urge to dig in the dirt, raise livestock, and participate in the ancient vocation that produced the first civilizations at the dawn of history. You don't have to grow up on a farm to experience farm living.

Further Reading

Anderson, Joan. *American Family Farm*. Minneapolis, Minn.: Econo-Clad Books, 1999.

Blackiston, Howland. *Beekeeping for Dummies*. New York: Hungry Minds, Inc., 2002.

Foster, Rory C. *I Never Met an Animal I Didn't Like*. New York: Franklin Watts, 2000.

Johnson, Sylvia A. *A Beekeeper's Year*. Boston, Mass.: Little, Brown and Company, 1994.

Kerswell, James. *Horses*. New York: Crescent Books, 2001.

Leffingwell, Randy. *Classic Farm Tractors*. Osceola, Wis.: Motorbooks International, 1993.

McBane, Susan. *How Your Horse Works*. Newton Abbot, UK: David and Charles, 1999.

Morse, Roger A., and Nicholas W. Calderone. *The Value of Honey Bees as Pollinators of U.S. Crops in 2000*. Ithaca, N.Y.: Cornell University, 2000.

Murphy, Dennis J., and Karen M. Hackett. *Children and Safety on the Farm*. University Park: Penn State University, 1997.

Nieson, Marc. *Barns*. Mankato, Minn.: Creative Education, 2002.

For More Information

www.campsilos.org

www.cyberspaceag.com

www.ext.vt.edu/resources/4h/virtualfarm/main.html

www.hoards.com

www.honey.com/kids/trivia.html

www.kidsarus.org

www.mda.state.mi.us/kids/pictures/rachel.html

www.national4-hheadquarters.gov

www.usda.gov/news/usdakids

www.4-hontario.ca

www.4husa.org

Publisher's note:
The Web sites listed on this page were active at the time of publication. The publisher is not responsible for Web sites that have changed their addresses or discontinued operation since the date of publication. The publisher will review and update the Web-site list upon each reprint.

Glossary

broody: Having to do with a hen that is ready to sit on eggs before they hatch.

centralization: Concentration in one, central location.

clutch: The number of eggs hatched by a bird at one time.

combined: Used a large harvesting machine to harvest crops.

commercialized: Applied profit-making principles to something.

corncrib: A ventilated building used for storing and drying grain.

derogatory: Expressing low opinion or negative criticism.

docile: Tame.

eclectic: Made up of elements from various sources.

elevator: A storehouse for grain that is equipped with a mechanism for taking in, lifting, and discharging the grain.

emaciated: Extremely thin, especially because of starvation or illness.

euthanize: To humanely kill an incurably ill or injured animal.

fallow: Left unseeded after plowing.

furrow: A narrow trench made by a plow.

geneticist: Someone who studies genetics, the factors involved with DNA and biological heritage.

horticulture: The science, skill, or occupation of cultivating plants.

imprint: To learn an attraction to members of the same species or substitutes very early in life.

legume: A plant that has pods as fruits and roots that bear nodules containing nitrogen-fixing bacteria.

metallurgist: Someone who studies metals.

nectar: Sweet liquid produced by flowering plants.

orchardist: Someone who owns or operates an orchard.

oxyacetylene torch: A torch that uses a mixture of oxygen and acetylene to cut and weld metal.

parlor: A special room in the barn where milking is done.

poults: Young fowl, especially turkeys.

precocious: More developed than expected at a given age.

progressive: Forward thinking.

pullets: Young female chickens that have not started to lay eggs.

silage: Animal fodder that is made by storing green plant material in a silo where it is preserved by partial fermentation.

stereotypes: Oversimplified ideas based on incomplete information held by someone about others.

surveyor: One who measures land to determine boundaries, elevations, and dimensions.

tandem axle: Two axles close together.

valedictorian: The student with the highest average in a graduating class.

Bibliography

Agriculture Talking Points. http://www.agday.org/planning/talkingpts.htm.

Barncats Incorporated. http://www.barncats.org.

Careers in Agriculture and Food Sciences. http://www.agriscience.ca/pages/e_stlounge.html.

Cornell Cooperative Extension, Genesee County. http://www.cce.cornell.edu/Genesee/4H/tractorsafety.htm.

Flottum, Kim. "Testing Honey." *Bee Culture,* March 2003.

Gardner, Elliott. *Changing Times*. Bath, N.Y.: Garreson Publishing, 2002.

John Deere. http://www.johndeere.com.

"Longing for the Farm." *Reader's Digest*, April 2005.

Louisiana Farm Bureau Federation. http://www.lfbf.org/member/facts.

Morse, Roger A., and Nicholas W. Calderone. *The Value of Honey Bees as Pollinators of U.S. Crops in 2000*. Ithaca, N.Y.: Cornell University Press.

Murphy, Dennis J., and Karen M. Hackett. *Children and Safety on the Farm*. University Park: Penn State University Press, 1997.

National Honey Board. "National Honey Board Funds Production Research Projects." Press release, February 25, 2005.

National Honey Board. http://www.honey.com/kids/trivia.html.

Penn State Ag Sciences. http://aginfo.psu.edu/radio/scripts/1005041.htm.

"Rural American Is Online." *Progressive Farmer*, February 2005.

Index

Picture Credits

Biographies

Author

Peter Sieling writes educational books, articles, and humorous essays. He owns Garreson Publishing Company and Garreson Lumber Company. He has written several books for Mason Crest Publishing. His articles appear in *Popular Woodworking, Sawmill and Woodlot Magazine, Bee Culture*, and *Christian Science Monitor*. Peter lives in upstate New York on a small farm with his family, numerous peafowls, chickens, and honeybees.

Series Consultant

Celeste J. Carmichael is a 4-H Youth Development Program Specialist at the Cornell University Cooperative Extension Administrative Unit in Ithaca, New York. She provides leadership to statewide 4-H Youth Development efforts including communications, curriculum, and conferences. She communicates the needs and impacts of the 4-H program to staff and decision makers, distributing information about issues related to youth and development, such as trends for rural youth.